'Mike opened his mouth, and very carefully nibbled the plant. For a moment he stood quite still.

"I can't believe it!" he exclaimed aloud. "It's marzipan."

And at that precise moment, he remembered what he had read on the packet. DON'T TELL ANYBODY, it had said. KEEP IT TO YOURSELF!'

When Mike discovers that he can grow sweets from a mysterious packet of seeds, he is suddenly very popular with almost everyone at school. Then nosy Angela starts asking awkward questions. If Mike isn't careful, she might discover his secret and ruin everything . . .

Also available by Alexander McCall Smith,
and published by Young Corgi Books:

ALIX AND THE TIGERS
SUZY MAGICIAN
THE TIN DOG

MIKE'S MAGIC SEEDS is one of a series of books especially selected to be suitable for beginner readers, BY MYSELF books.

Mike's Magic Seeds

Alexander McCall Smith

Illustrated by Kate Shannon

YOUNG CORGI BOOKS

For Jessica and Harriet de Bene

MIKE'S MAGIC SEEDS

A YOUNG CORGI BOOK 0 552 52476 X

Originally published in Great Britain by Young Corgi Books

PRINTING HISTORY

Young Corgi edition published 1988
Reprinted 1991

This book is set in 14/18 pt Century Schoolbook
by Colset Private Limited, Singapore

Young Corgi Books are published by Transworld Publishers Ltd., 61–63 Uxbridge Road, Ealing, London W5 5SA, in Australia by Transworld Publishers (Australia) Pty. Ltd., 15–23 Helles Avenue, Moorebank, NSW 2170, and in New Zealand by Transworld Publishers (N.Z.) Ltd., Cnr. Moselle and Waipareira Avenues, Henderson, Auckland.

Made and printed in Great Britain by
The Guernsey Press Co. Ltd., Guernsey, Channel Islands.

Chapter One

Mike saw the sign as he went round the corner. CLOSING DOWN SALE, it said. EVERYTHING MUST GO.

He stopped to look. He had never noticed the shop before, although he walked that way every day. Perhaps he had never seen it because it was so small – just one window with not very much in it. Perhaps he had always been looking the other way, or perhaps his eye had been caught by brighter, more exciting shops. Anyway, there it was – a tiny, dowdy little shop with one dirty window and a door that needed painting.

Mike felt in his pocket. Yes, he had some money; not very much, but a few coins nonetheless. If there was a sale on then everything would be cheap. He could always look. There was nothing wrong in just checking up. You never knew what you might find inside, and you'd never find it if you never looked.

Inside the shop there was only one light and everything seemed very dark. Mike blinked as his eyes got used to the darkness, and then, quite suddenly, a voice said, 'Yes? And what can I do for you?'

Mike gave a start. There, behind the counter, was an old man with a small pair of glasses perched on the end of his nose.

'Oh,' said Mike, sounding rather nervous. 'I saw that you had a sale on. I thought I'd see what you had.'

The shopkeeper peered at him. 'Yes. That's what the sign says. What would you like to buy?'

Mike was silent for a moment. He had no idea how to answer this question. As far as he could see, there was very little left in the shop. There were a few boxes, some of them closed, a pile of old gloves, a box of blunt pencils, one or two things that he couldn't quite tell the use of, a spare tube for a bicycle – but nothing that he would really want to buy.

'Well,' said the old man, now sounding rather impatient. 'Can't you make your mind up?'

'I don't know,' Mike said. 'I can't really see anything I want. And yet . . .'

'Ha!' snorted the shopkeeper. 'Another person who doesn't know what he wants. The world seems to be full of people like that.'

Mike looked about him, thinking that if he bought something quickly then he could get out of the shop and leave this rather strange man. No wonder he's closing down, he said to himself. If this is the way he speaks to his customers, then it would be very strange if he ever had any.

As he thought this, his gaze fell on a large wooden box perched on the highest shelf.

'That box,' he said, pointing to it.

'What have you got in that box?'

'I haven't the slightest idea,' the shopkeeper said grumpily. 'And I won't get it down unless you agree to buy what's in it. I'm not going to all the trouble of getting my ladder just to let you see it. People always ask for the things that are furthest away!'

Mike stared at the box. There was something about it that interested him. Who knew what was in it? It might be something valuable, or it might be something worthless. It might, of course, be something that he had always really wanted, or it could be something that he would never be able to use, or even to give away. He felt in his pocket and took out his coins.

'All right,' he said bravely. 'Here's my money. Is this enough to buy

whatever is in that box?'

The shopkeeper looked at the coins which Mike had put on the glass top of his counter.

'That's not very much,' he said. 'Haven't you got any more?'

Mike shook his head. He thought it was quite a lot of money, no matter what the shopkeeper felt. Why, there was enough there to go to a film and buy an ice cream to eat during the interval. Or there was enough to buy six or seven bars of chocolate. There was any number of things you could do with that much money.

'Oh, very well,' said the old man eventually. 'That'll have to do, I suppose.'

As he spoke, he scooped up Mike's

coins into his hand and plodded off to fetch his stepladder. Mike's heart was beating hard as the ladder was brought back. Why on earth, he asked himself, have I made such a silly decision? Whoever in his right mind would buy something he had never seen before? Would you?

Chapter Two

The shopkeeper put the box down on his counter. Then, taking a large red handkerchief out of his pocket, he gave the top of the box a good dusting. It had obviously not been touched for years, so thick was the layer of dust.

'It gets everywhere,' he said crossly. 'Dust! Dust! There's no escaping it.'

Mike said nothing. He was far too excited at what might be in the box to worry about a little dust.

'Please open it,' he said. 'I can't wait to see what I've bought.'

The shopkeeper peered at him and then, quite calmly, took off his spectacles and began to polish them with his red handkerchief.

'Patience, young man!' he said. Then he replaced his glasses on the end of his nose and gave the box a good shake. From the inside there came a strange sort of rattle – not a hard rattle or a soft rattle, but an odd, difficult-to-guess rattle.

'Go on,' Mike urged. 'Let's see what's inside.'

The shopkeeper looked at him

sharply, but this time did not say anything. Gingerly, as if he was worried that he might break whatever was in the box, he prised open the lid. Mike caught his breath as the box came open. Yes, there was something there – something square and brown.

'I see,' said the shopkeeper, smiling for the first time. 'And what do you think this might be?'

Mike watched as the shopkeeper held the object aloft.

'Yes,' said the old man. 'I remember now. I remember what I put in here.' He paused. 'You're going to be very disappointed, young man. Very disappointed indeed.'

Mike looked at the envelope which the shopkeeper held up.

'What's in it?' he said. The shopkeeper was right. He felt very disappointed. All the excitement seemed to have gone – who could get excited about an old envelope?

The shopkeeper handed the envelope to Mike.

'I hope you like gardening,' he said, laughing as he spoke. 'You've just bought a packet of seeds!'

Mike took the envelope from him and examined it. There were no pictures on the outside, showing you what sort of seeds they were. There was only a list of instructions about planting. And to think that he had spent not just half his money on the seeds, but all of it! He knew that he would be far too ashamed to tell

anybody – all his friends would laugh if they found out.

'Thank you,' he said to the shop-keeper.

'That's all right,' the old man replied. 'Are you sure you don't want anything else?'

'No,' said Mike firmly, although he really meant yes, he was quite sure he did not want anything else. One mistake, after all, was enough for one day.

When he got home, Mike sat in his room and looked glumly at the packet of seeds. Should I throw them away? he asked himself. There was no point in planting them – the garden was full enough of flowers and vegetables as it was.

Mike rose to his feet and threw the packet into the wastepaper bin. Then he sat down again and started to read, hoping that he would forget the whole matter. As he picked up the book his eye returned to the wastepaper basket. The discarded packet of seeds lay on top of some papers and he could just make out something printed

along the bottom. Gingerly rescuing it, he peered at the tiny print.

'Red seeds,' it said. 'Plant these on a Wednesday. Blue seeds: plant these on Tuesdays or Thursdays. White seeds: never plant these on any day but a Friday.'

And then, just under these instructions, a warning was printed in red: DON'T TELL ANYBODY! KEEP

IT TO YOURSELF! Mike turned the packet over in his hand. Very carefully he tore it open at the top. Inside, nestling at the bottom, were five or six large seeds. One of them was white and the rest were a variety of colours. Mike took out the white one and examined it carefully. It could be a sunflower, he thought; it was the right size for that.

'Today's Friday,' he said to himself. 'Exactly the right day for a white seed.'

Chapter Three

There was a place at the bottom of the garden where, for some reason, nothing ever seemed to grow. Mike's father had planted cabbages there one year, but they had never grown very well. Since then it had become covered with weeds and nobody paid much attention to it. That, thought Mike, is the place to plant my seeds.

Putting the white seed in his pocket, and tucking the rest away in the drawer in which he kept his socks, Mike went out into the garden. There was a hoe in the shed and he used this to clear a small patch of ground amongst the weeds. It was not very big – just enough to let the plant, whatever it was, grow without being smothered.

He put the seed into a shallow hole,

carefully covering it up with earth. Then, filling a watering can with water, he gave the ground around the newly planted seed a good soaking. It was the first time he had ever planted anything, and the fact that it was such a mysterious seed made him feel excited. He had no idea at all of what would grow, and this made it all the more thrilling.

Two days later, Mike went out into the garden to water the spot where he had planted the seed. As he reached the place, he noticed that there was something different about it. Some of the weeds had wilted and died and, in the middle, the earth seemed to have swollen.

Mike bent down to take a closer

look. Yes, there was no doubt that something was growing there. It was hard to believe that in such a short time the seed had grown so much, and yet there was the bulge in the earth. Whatever was growing underneath the ground was certainly rather strong. Perhaps it was a tree, a mighty tree like those that grow in the jungles of the Amazon. That

would be wonderful, Mike thought. It could be a giant of a tree with creepers hanging down from its branches and moss growing on its trunk. He could climb it and look down on the country-side for miles around. His tree would become famous and people would come to see it from far and wide.

Mike poured a generous helping of water on to the ground above the bulge.

'There,' he said. 'That should help you grow.'

As the water drained down into the ground, the soil seemed to give a little heave. It's almost breaking the surface, Mike thought. Tomorrow I'll have a plant.

Mike woke up early the next morning and went out into the garden immediately after breakfast.

'What are you doing out there?' his father asked suspiciously. 'I hope you're not doing anything to my cabbages.'

Mike did not tell his father what he was up to. Somehow he wanted to keep this to himself. He'll see it all soon enough, he said to himself. And then he wondered: he'll see what soon enough?

As soon as he walked out into the garden, Mike realized that his plant had grown. In the space of one night the seed had sprouted and a large, multi-coloured bush now stood where before there had been only weeds.

Mike caught his breath as he approached the bush. It was quite unlike any other plant he had ever seen before. To begin with, the one colour it was not was green, unlike all the other plants in the garden. Mike's plant, however, was red in some parts and yellow in others. The stalk, which was about as thick as his arm, was orange.

And then there were no leaves. At the end of each branch where you would expect to find the leaves, there were round knobs, rather like toffee apples but not quite as big. It was, Mike thought, the most extraordinary plant imaginable. But it was also very, very beautiful – the sort of plant that you want to stop and say 'hello' to, or 'How do you do?', or something friendly like that.

Mike reached out and felt his plant. It was not very smooth to the touch and yet it was not very rough. It felt rather like a dog's nose when it's dry. It also felt as if, with the slightest twist of the wrist, it would break.

And that is exactly what happened. The twig which Mike was touching came away in his hand, just like that, and he found himself holding a small piece of the plant. Lifting it to his nose, he sniffed at it. It smelled good. Mike turned it over in his hand and sniffed it again.

'I wonder,' he said to himself. 'Should I eat it?'

Now, there are a lot of people who would have said, 'No, don't eat it.' But what would you say?

Chapter Four

Mike did not make up his mind straight away. Putting the piece of plant into his pocket, he set off for school. It was difficult, of course, to think about much else that morning and several times he found himself having to answer a question that he had not really heard.

When the lunch break came, he could contain himself no longer. He had made up his mind. He would taste – just taste, mind you – a little bit of the plant. Not a large chunk – not a mouthful – just a nibble and definitely no more.

Finding a quiet place where nobody would disturb him, Mike took the plant out of his pocket. It still smelled as interesting as it had smelled that morning and it still felt as strange to the touch.

He raised the plant to his lips and touched it with his tongue.

'Hello, Mike. What are you doing?'

Mike spun round. It was one of his friends.

'Nothing,' he said. 'Nothing at all.'

'What's that you've got in your hand?' His friend peered at the plant, but was unable to see it very well.

'Nothing,' said Mike again, wishing his friend would go away. He could hardly believe what he had tasted when he licked the plant. Surely it couldn't be that! Surely not!

Mike's friend looked at him strangely. Then, to Mike's great relief, somebody called him and he walked away. Now, Mike thought, I can see if I was right.

Mike opened his mouth and very carefully nibbled the plant. For a moment he stood quite still.

'I can't believe it!' he exclaimed aloud. 'It's marzipan.'

And at that precise moment, he remembered what he had read on the packet. DON'T TELL ANYBODY, it had said. KEEP IT TO YOURSELF!

When he came home from school that day, the first thing Mike did was to go to the end of the garden to check his plant. It had not grown any more, but then it had not become any smaller. He broke off another piece, one of the round bits at the end of a branch, and took a bite of it. It tasted every bit as delicious as the small piece he had eaten that morning. He ate some more, and a little more after that, and then he went inside.

Back in his room, he opened his sock drawer and took out the seeds again. There were five left – all of them different. Mike chose one, a dark red seed which was a little smaller than the one which had produced the marzipan plant. I'll plant this now, he thought, and see what we get the day after tomorrow.

Mike spent the next two days wondering what he would find when his new plant came up. When at last it was time to check, he was prepared for anything, but what he saw still gave him a very great surprise.

Yes, there was something there, but it was much smaller than the marzipan bush. This time it was a spiky little plant, with deep green leaves on the

outside and a stick growing up the middle. The stick, which was dark brown, looked at first as if it was peeling, but when Mike looked more closely he realized it was not peeling, but flaky.

Dark brown and flaky! Could it be . . .?

Mike reached out and broke a segment off the top of the stick. It was soft and . . . melty. It was, of course . . . Well, what do you think it was?

It was chocolate flake!

If you have a marzipan bush and a chocolate flake plant in your garden, you should feel rather lucky. Mike certainly did. Some might be content with that and just sit back and enjoy being able to have these sweets whenever they feel like them. Mike, however, kept thinking of the three remaining seeds.

'I shouldn't be impatient,' he said to himself. 'I should keep the other seeds and only use them when I need them.' He knew this was the wise thing to do, but at the same time he could hardly wait to see what they would grow.

And so he planted them. On the right day for each seed he sowed them in a neat little row beside the marzipan bush and the chocolate flake plant. Then all he had to do was to wait.

Chapter Five

Three trees now grew beside the marzipan bush and the chocolate flake plant. They were all very small, but each one was most unusual. One was a coconut tree – not an ordinary coconut tree, but a coconut ice tree. Another was an almond tree –

sugared almonds, of course. And the third was a fig tree, which grew, at the tip of its tiny branches, the most delicious fig rolls.

Mike tended the plants carefully, picking only a few things from them each day. Yet although he did not take much, it was far more than he could ever eat himself. Deciding that he would give what was leftover to his friends, each day he took to school a bag full of pieces of marzipan, sugared almonds, and all the other things that the plants gave him.

'Where do you get it all from?' his friends asked, as they munched on the delicious sweets he gave them. 'Have you robbed a bank?'

Mike smiled. 'No,' he replied. 'Not a

single thing is stolen.'

'Well, tell us then,' his friends pressed. 'Don't be selfish.'

Mike would have loved to tell them, but he remembered what the packet had said and he feared that if he disobeyed, something terrible would happen to his marvellous plants. He could not bear the thought of not being able to go out into the garden and pick exactly what he wanted to eat. Imagine not being able to have chocolate flake whenever you felt like it! Imagine having to go out and buy sugared almonds!

Of course, being able to give away such delicious things made Mike very popular. Wherever he went, there were people who were only too happy to talk to him. Some of them offered to carry his books for him (he always said no) and others were always asking him round to their houses.

It was good to have so many friends. Each day, Mike could take his pick from the invitations he had received. Sometimes he would go with people to the snack bar near the school and eat ice cream with them. Sometimes he would go round to somebody's house and look at the things they had. One boy in his class, whose parents gave him just about everything (except for sweets), let him use his radio-controlled model plane. Mike had always wanted to fly one of these and it was every bit as much fun as he had thought it would be.

At parties, everybody seemed to be happy to talk to him. Other people had to sit about and hope that they wouldn't be left out: this never happened to Mike any more.

Having so many friends took up a lot of time, of course. Mike would have liked to have spent some time with his old friends, particularly with Tim whom he had known for years, but Tim did not seem to fit in with the new people Mike was seeing. When there were lots of people around, Tim just seemed to stand in the background and say nothing. He seemed to be less fun than the new people. They were always cracking jokes and coming up with ideas for things to do – Tim just wanted to do the things

that he and Mike had always done, and that didn't seem so exciting any more.

'Do you want to come to the quarry?' Tim asked Mike one afternoon. 'We could climb down the side. Remember the time we did that?'

Mike looked at his old friend.

'What's the point of that?' he asked. 'You just get down to the bottom then you have to climb up to the top again.'

'It's good fun,' said Tim. 'You used to like it.'

‘Used to,’ Mike said, shrugging his shoulders. ‘It’s not so good any more. Anyway, I’ve been asked over to Angela’s house.’

Tim turned away. Mike had not meant to be unkind to him, but life was just too exciting now to spend his time with people he’d known for so long.

Everybody wanted to know Angela. Her parents, who lived in a large house on the edge of the town, were extremely rich. The house had an indoor swimming pool (with a diving board), two tennis courts, and just about every game you could care to mention. When Angela held parties, there was more to eat and drink than at any other parties, and there were usually live bands as well.

When people heard that Mike was being invited to Angela's house, they were all rather jealous. Most of them were invited there very rarely, but Mike was now asked over just about every Saturday. It was a nice feeling knowing that you were going somewhere everybody else would love to go, but couldn't.

After a few weeks, Angela began to annoy Mike. Slowly he began to realize that she wasn't interested in him for himself, but that she wanted to be with him for another reason. It was difficult now to get away from her.

'How are you today, Mike?' Angela

enquired every morning. 'It's so nice to see you.'

'I'm all right,' Mike would reply, trying to walk faster so that Angela could not keep up.

'Can I walk with you?' Angela went on. 'I just love talking to you!'

Mike said nothing, trying to walk even faster, but Angela had long legs and found no difficulty in keeping up with him.

'Ah!' she said. 'I see you've got that bag with you. Would you mind if I had a little chocolate – just a little?'

And so it went on. Whenever he tried to be by himself, Angela would come up to him and try to talk to him. Mike knew that she didn't really like him, and this made him crosser and crosser. Angela, however, did not seem to notice, and Mike even heard her telling somebody that as she was his best friend she should have first pick of the things he brought in his bag.

'Mike,' Angela whispered one day. 'You can tell me, you know. I know how to keep a secret!'

'Tell you what?' Mike asked.

'You can tell me where you get all those good things from,' Angela went on. 'You must get them from somewhere.'

Mike felt cold inside. If Angela found out about his special plants, then that would be the end of them.

'I'm sorry,' he said. 'I'm busy. You'll have to talk to somebody else.'

He walked away, but later that day he saw Angela watching him. She was spying on him, he thought, and that made him feel very anxious indeed.

'She's going to spoil it all,' Mike said to himself. 'I'm sure of it.'

Chapter Six

Angela didn't give up. Whenever she saw Mike she would come up to him and quiz him about the source of all the delicious sweets.

'I promise I won't tell anyone else,' she pleaded. 'I promise, I promise!'

Mike knew that he couldn't trust

her. She was not the sort to keep a secret, and he suspected that the moment she knew, everyone else would know.

As he refused to tell her what she wanted to know, Angela became angrier and found it more difficult to pretend to like Mike. He heard her saying nasty things about him to other people, although to his face she was different.

Mike even noticed her looking over the gate of the house one afternoon,

and this gave him a fright. If she saw him going into the garden and coming back with a full bag, then she would realize what was happening. And that, he thought, would be the end of it all. DON'T TELL ANYBODY, the packet had said.

Eventually it came to a head. Mike had been out watering his plants one day and when he came into the house he heard voices from the kitchen. He went in to see who was visiting and there, sitting at the kitchen table, talking to his parents, was Angela.

'Oh, hello, Mike,' Angela said, smiling sweetly. 'I came to see you.'

Mike pursed his lips in anger.

'Well, Mike,' his father said. 'Aren't

you going to be polite to your visitor?'

Mike mumbled something which sounded as if it might have been hello and sat down at the table.

'Mike's very lucky,' Angela said brightly, glancing sideways at Mike as she spoke.

'Really?' Mike's mother said. 'Why

do you think he's lucky?'

Angela grinned at Mike. 'He always has so many good things to eat. Every day at school he seems to have a whole bag full of sweets like chocolate flake. Marzipan, too. Lots of it.'

Mike felt his heart stop. Oh no, he thought. This is it.

'Mike?' his father said. 'Is that true?'

Mike said nothing. He was staring at the floor. There was nothing to say.

'Well?' Mike's father said, sounding more puzzled. 'Haven't you got an explanation?'

Angela was still smiling. 'I've asked him again and again where he gets it all from,' Angela said. 'But he always refuses to tell me.'

There was a silence. Then Mike's father looked at his son severely and said: 'I think you've got some explaining to do.'

It was over. Mike knew that there was now no way out. He would have to tell them about his plants.

Quietly, Mike led them out of the house and to the place at the end of the garden where his plants had grown.

'There,' he said, not daring to look up. 'That's where I get everything.'

'Where?' Mike's father asked.

Mike looked up. His beautiful plants, so colourful and so generous, had withered. The marzipan plant was a little crumpled heap of dried

twigs; the chocolate flake plant had melted. The trees were lifeless sticks.

'He was lying,' Angela hissed. 'He wasn't telling the truth.'

Mike did not say anything. Turning round, he ran back to the house and locked himself in his room. He opened his drawer and took out the packet in which he had bought the seeds. Turning it upside down, he shook it. Nothing came out. He would never be able to find seeds like that again, never.

Or would he? What if he went back

to the shop? What if he went back and asked the old man if there were any more seeds for sale? It was always possible, after all, that the shopkeeper would have another packet.

'Yes?' said the shopkeeper, peering at Mike. 'Haven't I seen you before?'

'I bought something from you the other day,' Mike replied. 'I wondered . . .'

The shopkeeper stopped him. 'No,' he said, raising a hand. 'I'm not going to take it back. I'm sorry.'

'You don't understand,' protested Mike. 'I . . .'

The shopkeeper interrupted him again. 'I never take things back, even if they fall to bits the moment you leave the shop. I've never done so, and I never shall.' He paused. 'Anyway, I'm closing up for good tomorrow. This is the last day of the sale.'

'But I don't want you to take anything back,' Mike blurted out. 'I want some more!'

The shopkeeper looked astonished. 'More? More what, may I ask?'

Mike explained that he wanted some more of the seeds he had bought. The old man looked doubtful but agreed to take down the box and look inside. As he opened it, he shook his head.

'I'm sorry,' he said. 'It looks as if you're out of luck ... No, wait a moment. Yes, here we are. There are two loose seeds left. How much

money have you got?'

Mike turned out his pockets. It was very little.

'Mmm,' said the shopkeeper dubiously. 'That's not very much for two seeds. Seeds aren't cheap these days, you know.'

'Please,' said Mike.

The shopkeeper wrinkled up his nose.

'Oh, very well,' he said grudgingly. 'Here you are.'

Mike took the seeds and put them carefully in his pocket.

'Thank you very much,' he said, and then, just as he left the shop, he asked: 'Do you know what those seeds were – the ones you sold me last time?'

The shopkeeper nodded. 'Of course I know.'

Mike doubted this. 'Tell me then,' he challenged.

'Marzipan, chocolate flake, things like that,' said the shopkeeper vaguely. 'Now, off you go. I'm closing up!'

Chapter Seven

Once the remnants of the old plants had been cleared away, the ground was ready for the new seeds. Mike put them in carefully, covering them with just the right amount of earth and watering them straight away. He could hardly wait to find out what would grow. The seeds themselves looked different from the first lot, and so the plants would no doubt be different too. He hoped that there would be more chocolate, but really anything would do.

He found it difficult to concentrate at school and he even failed to notice how nasty Angela was being.

'You're not going to get away with this,' she said bitterly. 'You can't think I'd be fooled so easily!'

Mike just smiled. When the new plants grew, he would be more careful. He would no longer bring any bags full of good things to school; he would give them to his friends in secret. Angela, he hoped, would never find out.

Without the bags of sweets, things seemed different. There were fewer people around him all the time, and some of the people who seemed keenest to know him just drifted away. They weren't rude to him or anything like that, it was just that they didn't seem interested.

'By the way,' Mike said to Tim, 'would you like to go out to the quarry again one day?'

Tim smiled. 'Of course,' he said. 'Any time you want.'

When he got home from school, Mike went straight to the garden and looked at the ground where he had planted the seeds. Nothing had yet appeared. He went down on his knees

and looked at the soil above the seeds. Was there a bulge? No. At least, not yet.

Next morning, he went out the moment it was light. Surely something would have grown by now. The seeds had been in the ground long enough.

There was nothing there. Mike now began to feel worried. He fetched a watering can and gave the ground a good soaking. This afternoon, he told himself. Something will have grown by then.

But that afternoon, when he went back to the garden, there was still no sign of growth. There was no bulge in the ground and no little cracks to show that something was trying to push its way through. His heart sinking, Mike watered them again and went away. He tried not to think too much about the seeds, knowing that it was always best to forget about something you really wanted to happen, although this was very hard. The thought of his lovely marzipan bush kept coming back to him, and the taste of the chocolate flake still lingered . . .

There was nothing the next day, nor the next. The day after that, it was just the same. Nothing had grown. There was only the empty ground, with the weeds at the edge. They, of course, just grew bigger and bigger.

That could have been the end of the story of Mike and the magic seeds, but it wasn't. Ten days later, when Mike had given up all hope of anything happening, his father said something which made his heart leap with joy.

'Mike,' his father began, 'you know that place in the garden where you grew those funny dried-up plants, the ones that died?'

Mike nodded.

'Well,' said his father, 'you seem to be getting something else down there. I noticed something growing when I was out there today. Should we go and take a look?'

Mike and his father made their way out into the garden. Mike hardly dared imagine what he would see, but he knew that whatever it was, it would be most unusual.

'There,' said his father. 'Two

plants. And I think I can tell what they are.'

Mike looked down at the ground. The plants were very small, but they were definitely just where he had planted the seeds.

'Yes,' said Mike's father. 'There's no doubt about it. You've got a couple of cabbages. Well done!'

Cabbages! Mike looked at the plants again and realized that his father was quite right. Cabbages!

And that, again, could have been the end of the story of Mike and the magic seeds. Once again, though, it wasn't.

Mike watched his cabbage plants grow. They were exactly the same as his father's, green and very dull. He thought of rooting them up and throwing them away, as the one thing that the house did not need was more cabbage. This would have been too much effort, however, and Mike was no longer interested in gardening.

Then, as he sat in his room, the thought came into his head: Why not look at those cabbages again? Just one more look?

Mike went out into the garden. He

could see that the cabbages were still there and there did not seem to be anything wrong with them.

'Should I eat one?' he said to himself. Then he laughed. 'No. Eat a raw cabbage?'

But would a taste matter? Just one little taste? He could always spit it out if it tasted too bad.

Mike bent down and picked a small piece of one of the cabbage leaves and gingerly licked it. Then he knew, and it seemed as if all the bells of heaven were ringing out at once.

Green mint chocolate.

If you would like to receive a Newsletter about our new Children's books, just fill in the coupon below with your name and address (or copy it onto a separate piece of paper if you don't want to spoil your book) and send it to:

The Children's Books Editor
Young Corgi Books
61-63 Uxbridge Road,
Ealing
London W5 5SA

Please send me a Children's Newsletter:

Name..

Address...

....

....

All Children's Books are available at your bookshop or newsagent, or can be ordered from the following address:
Corgi/Bantam Books,
Cash Sales Department,
P.O. Box 11, Falmouth, Cornwall TR10 9 EN

Please send a cheque or postal order (no currency) and allow 60p for postage and packing for the first book plus 25p for the second book and 15p for each additional book ordered up to a maximum charge of £1.90 in UK.

B.F.P.O. customers please allow 60p for the first book, 25p for the second book plus 15p per copy for the next 7 books, thereafter 9p per book.

Overseas customers, including Eire, please allow £1.25 for postage and packing for the first book, 75p for the second book, and 28p for each subsequent title ordered.